BIG
and little
On the Farm

by Dorothy Donohue

A Golden Book • New York
Golden Books Publishing Company, Inc.,
New York, New York 10106

BIG CHICK

little chick

BIG COW

little ca/f

BIG CAT

little kitten

BIG SHEEP

little lamb

BIG DUCK

little duckling

BIG HORSE

little foal

BIG GOOSE

little gosling

BIG GOAT

little kid

little piglet

BIG HUMAN

little baby